In The Garden
Of Moonlight

By

Cee McAdams

WingSpan Press

Published in the United States and the United Kingdom by WingSpan Press, Livermore, CA

The WingSpan name, logo and colophon are the trademarks of WingSpan Publishing.

ISBN 978-1-63683-007-0 (pbk.)
ISBN 978-1-63683-993-6 (ebk.)

First edition 2021

Printed in the United States of America

www.wingspanpress.com

1 2 3 4 5 6 7 8 9 10

QUOTES

"That's all we expect of man, this side of the grave: his good is – knowing he is bad."

Robert Browning

ADVICE FROM A HORSE: "Take life's hurdles in stride...loosen the reins...be free spirited...keep the burrs from under your saddle...carry your friends when they need it...keep stable...gallop to greatness."

Llan Shamir

"It's a new dawn, it's a new day, it's a new life..."

Nina Simone

For Travis

Table Of Contents

The Presidents Departure 1

Skedaddled.. 9

Serial Killer At Broken Rock Bog............................21

Transformation..27

The Carousel 31

Oh Woh Is He 37

Track Of The Kookaburra 45

In The Shadow Of Evil – The Introduction.........51

In The Shadow Of Evil 53

...And So I Write... 99

THE PRESIDENT'S DEPARTURE

Our club had been growing and doing quite well until he came and took over. One day he announced to the rest of us that he was going to be the president because he was more qualified to be the leader. We all stared in disbelief, each convinced that the president had to be appointed or elected but he did not know that our club had rules.

From the very first day he took over, chaos reigned. Nothing seemed to please him. He would start honking early in the morning before most of us could wake up and get the blood flowing through our feathers. He would strut around and find things to complain about. He wrote lots of memos and expected all of them to be followed to the letter. His name was Shady, a honker, and he was the president of the Barn & Fowl Club. Of course he appointed himself and felt that he could do that since he was the house pet and thought himself superior to the rest of us...we had quarters in the barn...he had his own room in the house and his own pond.

In the Garden of Moonlight

One day, Spireau, the senior rooster, had finally had enough. He called us all together and told us his plan.

About once a week, a man from the Feed & Seed would come and deliver feed. Mostly we went about our scratching and the ladies with little chicks went about their clucking and tending of the little ones. Today Spireau had decided that when the truck left the barn, Shady would be on it. We knew that we would have to grab him, tie him up and make sure that he would make no noise.

We fashioned a small cage out of wire that had been removed from the bales of hay, then we put a little hay around the sides so that Shady could not see out and no one would be able to see in. We had worked on this the evening before so everything would be ready when he marches out to the barn to start playing the Gestapo leader.

 Our secretary was a little lady named Zell, who was just naturally a busy-body. She always felt that the rest of us didn't get something right and felt put-upon to run around and spread her version of what had happened or what she thought was going to happen next. This morning while we were waiting for the feed truck to arrive, Zell was having a conversation with

Shady. We held our collective breath, hoping that she would not spill the beans about our plan to ship him off in the truck. What we did not know was that she was actually distracting him while we readied our makeshift cage.

The truck arrived and the driver unloaded the sacks of feed. While the driver went to the house to get his papers signed, we grabbed Shady and hurriedly stuffed him in the little cage. He struggled but had no time to honk because we wrapped his bill with string, not hard enough to hurt him but tightly enough to keep him quiet. Then we put him and his cage in the truck and covered it with some of the feed bags that were already there. Soon he would be on his way and we could get back to running our club. The truck left with Shady and that was the last we would see of him, or at least we hoped...it seems Ol Shady had other plans.

The truck driver returned to his store which was located near a mostly empty, mostly rundown mall. The driver unloaded and cleaned his truck everyday when he finished all of his deliveries. When he removed the feed sacks and saw this little cage, he didn't know what to make of it; nevertheless, he lifted it off the truck and sat it on the ground but when he opened it, out wobbled Shady, mostly falling over because his feet were tied together, tossing his head around, trying to get the string off his bill. The driver, totally baffled as to how this goose got on his truck, knelt down and untied him. As soon as the strings were removed, Shady began honking as loudly as he could. Ol Shady was totally outraged but grateful that no one could see his legs quivering. This had proven to be quite an ordeal for him.

There were a few stores that were trying to stay in business in this once thriving mall so the fountain was still operating. Apparently Ol Shady could smell the water so he took flight and landed near the entrance. Now all he had to do was find a way inside.

As luck would have it, someone just happened to be leaving and Shady rushed in and went straight to the fountain. Water never looked so good or tasted so refreshing so Shady strolled around inside the fountain enclosure for several long minutes and pondered his situation. He was far from home and away from what used to be his home and his friends. He had no idea how he was going to eat. What will happen to this water when the mall closes for the night? Where would he find more water? It began to dawn on him that perhaps he had over-estimated his importance and the club members had given him this little send-off to remind him.

Now he wondered how could he get back home and to his special place, his very own little pond which he realized he wanted to share with the other honker, a rather handsome female. He didn't really need to be president nor was he planning any kind of revenge. If he could just figure out how to get back home, he would apologize to the others, mend his ways and hope that they would allow him to be a part of the club but explain that he had no further interest in being president. It would be an humbling experience no doubt, but when you are a goose, injured pride hardly seems worth getting one's feathers all a-flutter.

The next morning, very early, Shady realized that he was ravenous but that he had made it through the night. Even though he had become somewhat of an attraction and enjoyed the attention, he knew that it was time to get out of the fountain and start on his journey. He took one last drink and held his head under the water for a few glorious minutes and then off he went. At first he could not find a way out. He went down long hallways in both directions but could find no way to escape the mall. Finally he heard a noise. It sounded like doors opening on the other end of the mall...he hurried in that direction.

In the Garden of Moonlight

It was in fact, the maintenance crew or the grounds crew or whatever they were called, reporting for work and he made a mad dash toward the exit.

Just in case no one saw him coming, he began honking as loudly as he could to create as much of a commotion as possible. Several heads turned his way, then some of them went to see what was causing such a ruckus and to see if perhaps they could help. Ol Shady waddled up to the door and waited for someone to open it. As soon as it was open, out he went, took a few running steps and then lifted into the air.

Shady traveled almost half of the day before he finally saw what looked like familiar territory. He could not believe that he had lost his bearings and had headed in the wrong direction many times. He swooped down and landed near what he hoped was still his home. He was hungry, thirsty and exhausted. He wanted to run to his own little pond but thought he had better get the unpleasant business of facing the others over with while he still had the strength and only semi-queasy nerves.

He moseyed into the barnyard and saw Zell, Spireau and the others. First he studied the ground for a long moment to summon his courage, and then he began to explain to them that he had been wrong and asked to be forgiven. Mostly, he just wanted to belong to their little club...he was resigning as president. All was quiet. No one moved or uttered a sound. Finally Zell walked over to him and welcomed him back. The others then followed. There was much laughter and hugs all around. Then Spireau asked Shady if he would like to be their emissary...he could go to the farmer and speak for them whenever they had troubles, requests or just simple concerns. He anxiously agreed and there were smiles all around. He was grateful to be accepted but mostly he was thrilled to be back home. Now he could spend his time basking in the sun, swimming in his little pond and pursuing the other honker, a really handsome female.

WELCOME TO BEARDSLEY

SKEDADDLED

The Pre-cursor

This story is about a town of unfriendly politicians who had to be taught a lesson about how to treat their animal neighbors. It involves a much-disputed area located at the edge of town and the mayor and his cohorts want to take over this lushly green area and turn it into a dog park. They claim that the present occupants, the gophers, are not properly tending the area and that they should be removed. Needless to say, the gophers objected and the uprising began.

The town is called BEARDSLEY. It is not an unusual town although it is run, albeit very badly, by a city council and an unusually incompetent mayor. Before it is all said and done, the mayor and his council will have to leave town to escape the wrath of the gophers.

SKEDADDLED

All around us, we heard the noises, human noises. We had heard them before but not like this. We didn't know if this meant trouble or just the same nosy humans trying to spy on our home. We thought it best to go about our daily business but keep an eye on the humans, just in case we needed to take some type of action.

We have been here in our Gopher Town for many years, living in peace with our human neighbors. In fact, we were here long before this village of Beardsley was established. Our town goes on for miles but all underground so our human neighbors cannot trip over our gardens or step on our little ones.

Our territory has expanded over time but not far enough to tread on our neighbors to the south; however, our neighbors to the West say they are feeling cramped and want us to move over. What they really want is for us to sit quietly while they take part of our homeland for a recreation area for their dogs...we say we're not going.

In the Garden of Moonlight

Down here, we have not only streets but super-highways...we can travel for miles to visit or just to take a look around. We do not build bridges or dams and we do not invade our neighbors. They, on the other hand, have plans to invade our territory and we will not take it lightly. It's time to gather our forces and prepare to defend our home.

The humans decided to get an early start. They were coming with their heavy machinery with plans to knock down bushes so that the small trees would grow. Everywhere they saw signs of openings to our undergrown paradise, they decided they would close and bury us underground. We have several doors and windows with which to escape as well as scouts and lookouts. They may have believed that they were sneaking in on us but we heard them coming for miles and we were waiting for them.

The mayor was the first to arrive. He was a grumpy little fellow, about 5 foot 8, something resembling a caterpillar growing on his lip. He had a rather large belly but always looked as if he was going to his own funeral. Today he was dressed in one of his finest suits and a tie loud enough to cause serious inner ear damage.

He stepped out of his limo, took a look around and finally spotted me. I stood very still as he approached. He was speaking to me as if I was the intruder but I said nothing, only listened to him spout off about how this area was needed and that he would be willing to give us time to move elsewhere. After all, he was the mayor...it was his decision and that the planning commission would have to follow his orders. He did not want to cause us any harm but would if we forced his hand..."and by the way, when would we be departing from the area"? Sooner rather than later, he threatened.

I told him that we would be leaving as soon as he grew taller and lost some of that protuberance, or whenever he was invited back for tea, whichever came first. Well the mayor did not take kindly to having his authority questioned or meeting with any objections whatsoever since he ran the town with an iron fist and an empty head. Most, if not all of the town council, consisted of relatives and he bullied them into doing his bidding...he expected no less from the town gophers. He stomped off in huff.

I could see the machinery but all of it was silent at the moment. The mayor had only moved it into place to have it ready at a moment's notice. This gave us time to marshal our resources. I hurried back into the burrow and called an emergency meeting. 'We should not wait until tomorrow,' I suggested...'we have time before the sun sets today to give them our message and then prepare for their reply tomorrow.' All agreed.

Shortly after the meeting was adjourned, we

gathered a few supplies and headed toward the home of the police chief. He lived in a house that was all wood and was the closest to our village. We started small and only gnawed a few holes in his garage, then filled it with his own garbage: a bottle here, a can there. Next we cut and twisted his phone lines so that he would probably reach Indonesia before he could call the mayor or anyone else for help.

The house on the other side of our village belonged to the mayor's cousin and was a member of the town council. She lived in a house that had once been occupied by she and her husband but he was now the dearly departed and the house was more run-down than not. She was so busy with her duties on the council that she mostly neglected the house so there were several areas that offered possible ingress. We did not wait for an invitation but we left her with a very explicit message we knew she would relay to the mayor.

The mayor lived on the other side of town and the farthest from our village so we had to hurry if we were going to get the job done and get back to our burrow before night. We had a very special message planned for the mayor but when we reached his house, we found brick and no way of getting inside. We looked around for a few minutes and at last we discovered a storage shed. It was not a very good target but it offered the best option at the moment...we hurried over to it to have a look.

When we reached the shed, we discovered that it was not at all like the house. No brick could be found which made it easier for us. There were cracks around the sides and we took the liberty of expanding them. We had borrowed a bit of fuel from the mayor's heavy equipment which we liberally poured on the brush and other debris we had gathered, formed a line of debris straight to the mayor's door and poured on a bit of fuel. Then we scurried back to our village.

By the time we returned home, the shadows were growing long and it was getting close to dark. We still had chores to do...each night now we have to make sure to fortify our home to keep out intruders of all kinds. We have learned a trick or two from our human neighbors... although we know nothing of technology, we have learned to be crafty and to use the resources around us. We have gathered a few cans and other metal objects that will make noise if something or someone breaches one of our entryways.

As usual, we took turns at sentry duty but fortunately nothing happened. The night passed without a single bang, rattle or even a squeak. We took a look around and found that our traps had not been disturbed so we cautiously went about our day, cognizant of the fact that the mayor's heavy equipment could roar to life at any moment.

It took about 12 hours before we received news that the mayor had called an emergency meeting. The police chief, the cousin of the mayor and a couple of others, had things to report. The police chief was the first to speak. He told those gathered that someone had cut holes in the side of his house and had so badly mangled his phone lines that he is still without the use of his phone. Further, there was every indication that this was the work of the gophers. Something has to be done.

The mayor's cousin loudly proclaimed that someone or something had been to her house as well...she would never leave trash lying around... it was a fire hazard! Besides that, the burglars or whomever, had brazenly left her a message that they would be back to thank her for the use of the hammer and the saw. "I now have a hole just underneath the back steps and a new trapdoor I neither want or need. How could this happen right under the nose of the police department"?

The mayor was instantly on his feet and pounding his gavel. "Quiet! I TOO had a visit from someone or more to the point, those blasted gophers! Did anyone see or hear anything? They were at my house and it is amazing that the house didn't burn down...there was the smell of fuel all over the place! I have had enough! Time to take the fight to them...they have got to go. Meeting adjourned." Then he banged his gavel and rushed out of the room.

Around midday, the mayor and his driver with the long, pointed ears, made their appearance at our village. The mayor, dressed in a splendid dark grey suit with silver stripes, with a tie that had more flowers than an arboretum, stepped out of his limo looking sour as if his lunch had not gone down well. He marched up to us, pointed a stubby finger and said; "leave or we will bury you...you've got 1 day." Then he marched back to his limo and they drove away.

This time we knew he meant it. We held a meeting and decided that we had to use all or most of the adults in our burrow if we were going to defeat the mayor and his minions. No matter what, we were not going to leave our home.

Not far from our village there is a large patch of vines with small green leaves and little white flowers...humans know this as poison ivy. It causes no harm to us but to the humans it will be a rather unpleasant experience to touch it. We are arranging just such a meeting of vines and humans. Of course we are going to disguise it but ultimately the disguise will fail and the fun will begin.

In the Garden of Moonlight

This morning, the sky was marbled, the clouds sort of streaked as if they were trying to decide to darken and send rain or just keep us in suspense for a few hours. We had no time to waste cloud-watching. There were several small groups of us gathering the vines to take back to our village to grind and blend with grass, jasmine and sand. Then we have to carefully distribute it among the human homes and the mayor's office, especially the town council chambers.

We worked most of the day distributing the little packets of ground vines. We put some in the mayor's limo, bedroom, bathroom and kitchen. We sprinkled it in the home of his cousin, everywhere we thought she would touch. We generously spread it around the police chief's house but did not go to his police headquarters. The rest of the town council received their share but none of them will be the wiser until it's too late. We did not forget the heavy equipment.

When we returned to our burrow, we were all exhausted. Humans go home and have a martini or two...we just go home and try to find a quiet place to lie down and rest, maybe get a nap. Sleep eluded most of us because we were on constant alert. Some of us just perched precariously on small boulders or underneath bushes, hidden from view, in case any of the humans passed by.

We were suddenly startled awake from a short nap by an ear-piercing, blood-curdling scream. It had come from the police chief's house or so we thought, but there were screams and moaning coming from several houses near our burrow. Humans seem to pour out of doors all around us, scratching and clawing at their clothes. We knew that our little gifts had been found and had hit the spot(s).

People were running and screaming. Some were driving way too fast...dust was flying...dogs were yelping...a few dogs were running alongside and others were chasing after the humans. It was quite a sight!

We were all hugging and dancing in celebration but kept a cautious eye for anyone who might decide to toss us a last-minute surprise on his way out of town.

Nothing more was heard from the humans. We were looking into the dying rays of the evening sun on the first evening of the humans' exodus. We have neither seen nor heard anything more from the mayor and his heavy equipment is sitting idle and gleaming dully in the evening light. For now, Beardsley is nearly deserted and we have Gopher Town all to ourselves. The dog park will just have to wait.

SERIAL KILLER AT
BROKEN ROCK BOG

Whomever started the rumor that catesbeiana were grumpy never met Mr. DeLumpy. He wasn't exactly the friendliest Rana around the bog but not really a bad guy. He would just sit all day long, grabbing rays whenever they were available and then take a dip or have a snack whenever he needed one.

One day Mr. DeLumpy was trying to get a nap just as the sun was taking its final bow of the day, sometimes referred to as twilight, when suddenly there was the most awful, ear-splitting chorus of off-key singing he had ever heard. What could be causing such a ruckus? He hopped along the edge of the pond and tried to see who or what had dared to disturb his evening nap...then he saw them, lots of Gryllidae and a few others he could not identify right away. In his deep resonant voice, he asked politely; 'please try to sing a little more softly – I'm trying to get a nap in the fading light of the evening...try to be a little more considerate.'

In the Garden of Moonlight

The singing ceased but for only a moment, then started up again even louder than before...a few others from a neighboring bog had joined in. This was just a bit too much for Mr. DeLumpy... he gave up on his nap and prepared to go on a killing spree.

Mr. DeLumpy was a magnificent jumper; he could travel great distances with a single stride but he preferred to conserve his energy and have his snacks and other delicacies come to him, so the very idea of having to work so hard just to be able to enjoy his nap only made his tongue itch. His normally sedate personality became riled and he grew grouchy and cantankerous. He mumbled to himself as he readied his plan to put a stop to this vile obnoxious disturbance.

Mr. DeLumpy could hardly contain his nervousness, just thinking about what he was about to do. Nevertheless, it was necessary. He tried to be a good guy and asked the neighbors nicely to hold the singing down to a soft roar but he was ignored. More than that, he was mocked and this he simply would not tolerate.

He decided that he would take the long way around the bog and try an ambush on the miscreants. It would serve them right to have no time to explain or try to escape. The only problem was that Mr. DeLumpy had no previous experience in planning a sneak attack...he had always simply waited until the right moment and slurp! It was gone, whatever had the misfortune of getting too close. Now he was not only going to have to re-structure his entire modus operandi but re-tool his combat skills. This is either going to be really tuff or great fun down at the old bog.

Mr. DeLumpy thought it over and decided that he knew only one way to go about this business and that was to get it done. He waited until the sun dipped below the horizon and the singing had kicked into high gear, then he puffed up his chest and started toward it.

He did not want to scare them off by doing his usual long gallop so he tried with all his might to take shorter jumps. He landed beside a small group of little green Cicadidae and flick! slurp! gulp! and that was the end of all of them except one that managed to escape.

He was about to move a bit farther down the bog but suddenly realized that the singing had ceased. He waited a few minutes to see if it was going to start up again but it did not. He had no doubt destroyed the sentries and the one that got away went to warn the others. Feeling slightly disappointed, he made his way back to his favorite spot and decided that he would try again the following evening when that horrible singing started up again. This time, he would be more careful.

Things were fairly quiet the rest of the evening and Mr. DeLumpy was able to get a good night's sleep. He awoke feeling chipper but decided to skip his usual morning routine of exercising his chords to get his day started...he did, however take his usual morning dip. The water felt cool and gave him the sense that all was well at the bog. He had not forgotten his exploits of the previous evening and secretly relished the idea of doing it again, only with more success...that had only been a trial run.

Two nights went by and no loud singing. Mr. DeLumpy felt that he could finally relax and enjoy the cool quiet of the evenings. He would sit on his favorite rock and revel in the slightly damp mossy aroma of the bog. He would exercise his vocal chords and feel impressed with the sound of them. Then one evening, just as the sun was setting, all of his expectations dissolved...the peace and serenity of the bog was shattered by the loudest and most obnoxious singing yet.

Mr. DeLumpy could no longer contain himself... he sprang into action right away. How dare these

Cicadidae and all of the other annoying little objections disturb his peaceful mood! He didn't even bother to formulate a plan...he just rushed off in the direction of that awful singing.

When he reached the first bunch of them, he all but took a deep breath and inhaled the lot of them, one after the other...then moved on. He found several others trying to escape but to no avail...flick, slurp and that was the end of them. By the time he reached the far end of the bog, he was feeling rather stuffed but knew he could not stop. He found several little green ones and thought they were especially delicious...flick, slurp, gulp.

Mr. DeLumpy sat very still and listened. He could hear no sound of anything...no movement and no singing. He returned to his favorite spot on his rock, puffed up his chest and fell asleep feeling full and satisfied.

Mr. DeLumpy was so full of Cicadidae and so happy that there were no noises to disturb his evening nap that he failed to hear the extremely slow and quiet movement of Mr. Ophidia, who happened to be looking for a late evening snack. He made no noise whatsoever and had Mr. DeLumpy in his grasp before he could bound away. The last sound that Mr. DeLumpy heard was faint off-key singing from way on the other side of the bog.

TRANSFORMATION

I walked along the narrow track, hardly more than a trail, which led to the creek about a mile from the place where I spend most of my days, a place I no longer call home but a place to get in out of the rain. I could smell the rain in the air which blended with the other smells of the woods. I can't say that it excited my senses because nothing resembling life happened to me anymore...I simply plodded along. Like most days, it was one of those mornings not worth waking up to; I felt listless, lethargic, resentful, depressed and totally dead inside. As I rounded the curve in the trail, I saw a small animal that appeared to be kneeling. As I got closer, I could see that it was a fawn, struggling to stand but its front legs were unable to support him. I looked around for his mother but nothing was in sight; she had either been killed or had abandoned it. Still I approached with caution. It was so small, hardly more than 8 or 9 pounds. I sat on the ground and lifted it onto my knees. My heart had grown calluses and many months ago, I tuned-out, shut down, closed up shop and moved away, but the sight of this little fawn caused the heavy drapes to pull aside and let in enough light to soften a callus or two. I could

27

In the Garden of Moonlight

hear thunder now and knew that the clouds would open up any minute. This little critter would surely drown or be eaten by a predator, so I picked him up gently and carried him back to the place that is no longer a home, placed him on the floor and tried to decide what to do with him, so small, weak and all but helpless; I suppose the first order of business is to feed him, then try to help him walk.

I looked around the place that was no longer home and discovered that I had nothing to feed such a tiny guest. I had to get into the village to find food for him and some way to feed and water him so I made him a place in the corner and covered him with a blanket. I hoped that he would be alright until I returned.

I bought some hay and ground corn and wondered if this would work long enough to keep him alive until he was old enough to feed himself. For days and days, I fed him chopped timothy grass, powdered milk I blended with wheat germ and coconut milk, which I fed to him through a small funnel, finely ground corn and an occasional banana. I made him braces of cardboard and duct tape. I put him in a tub of warm water and massaged his legs everyday. I gave him his own water bottle which he drank from enthusiastically. When I exhausted my nurse-maiding skills, I tried being a bad mother and yelled at him to walk on his own. This only brought a sad look from him but one day, while I was out getting more supplies, he did indeed decide to try walking on his own. When I opened the door, he came over to meet me. I felt almost human again as more calluses melted away. I think I heard myself laugh out loud. That day, I removed the make-shift braces – he wouldn't need them anymore. Now I had to think of a name for him.

I decided to call him Pocket...he had gained a pound or two but still very small and could almost fit into my jacket pocket. He went everywhere with me. Sadly, I realized that I was depriving him of the one thing he wanted and needed most, the ability to run and jump into puddles and dance around in the forest; I had to make a conscious effort not to pick him up so that he could enjoy his new freedom.

Pocket grew taller, ran faster and started jumping over almost everything. Watching Pocket grow made the mundane seem like the extraordinary. I no longer dreaded waking up, knowing that I would only feel lonely, depressed and miserable, but instead embraced each new day. My rage-fueled tantrums dissolved into quiet chats with Pocket. I have fixed up the old homestead – new doors and windows, a new coat of paint, even a new roof; it now feels like a home for Pocket and for me. We take long walks to the creek and on some days, look around for his mother; at other times, we reminisce about the day I found him and the day he transformed me.

THE CAROUSEL

The horses were restless. They paced and circled and pawed the ground. They stood underneath the trees in silence and then they would walk in circles, first each in his own thoughts and then two by two, muttering to each other. They would go over to the food bins and then eat nothing, silently chewing on imaginary hay. Finally, Beau, the youngest one of them said: "we cannot go on this way...there has to be a way out of this...we just have to put our heads together and come up with the right solution." They all stopped, stared at Beau and nodded in silent agreement. So Ben, the oldest, decided to assume the role as leader and called them all together. They did indeed put their heads together, proposing and rejecting one idea after the other, but at last, Ben declared the meeting over...they had come up with a plan. As soon as he finished speaking, they all nodded and instantly began to feel better.

The circus was coming to town and the horses knew that the farmer would rent them out for the carousel and they were all frantic. Each of them remembered what had happened the last time and wanted no part of that experience again. Ben had been spared because he had been ill the day the circus began. Now he decided that he would assume the responsibility of saving the others from what might be another near tragedy.

They lived with a farmer on a farm so remote that there were no other farms or ranches or houses within 10 miles. There was abundant grass and water and also creeks that were frequently dry, that ran for miles and led to no place in particular. There were hills with craters carved into them by Mother Nature when she decided to have one of her tantrums, where the horses would hide whenever there was a storm if they were too far away from the barn. The horses could only surmise that the farmer knew nothing about these little hidey-holes because none of them had bothered to discuss their existence with him and was not about to take him into their confidence at this point. One such hiding place was a bit larger than the others and this was, Ben decided, the ideal place to hide for a few hours or longer if necessary.

It was Saturday, the day the circus was to begin. The horses were up early, before the sun could emerge from underneath the blanket of cloud and announce a new day. They had eaten breakfast and were ready to leave around 5, before the farmer could come for them. They had their plan all set, details all worked out, extra food stashed in the hiding place and were convinced that they had done everything they could do. Ben, their leader, was the first out of the barn. He did not run but walked at a quick pace so as not to raise suspicion just in case the farmer happened to be looking out of the window, and made sure the others followed suit. If the farmer saw them running away toward the secret hiding place, that would ruin everything and all of their planning would be for naught.

In the village, about 20 miles from the farm, the circus owner was getting ready, setting up the last of the displays so that the circus could begin on time. The only thing left to do was set up the carousel. Of course in this circus, the carousel was made up of real horses, usually about 10 but frequently 10 horses were unavailable so 8 was the chosen number. This morning, the wheels had been oiled, the calliope was playing, the workers were all milling around in a hum-drum mood, but no horses stood at the ready. The circus owner ran around in circles, shouting orders to anyone and everyone at once, panting and perspiring, but no one could find even one horse for the carousel. Out of desperation, the circus owner decided to use other animals and ordered them to all be rounded up and made ready, but there were no tigers, lions, bears or elephants...not a goat, a gopher or even a dog could be found.

The owner thought this most peculiar but was unable to explain it and certainly unwilling to accept it. He returned to his office in a foul mood, stomping and snorting, and then sat down to ponder this mystery.

After much contemplating and head-scratching, he realized that there could be no circus without animals. He wondered out loud whether or not his mistreatment of the animals had finally forced them all to revolt, leaving the humans to jump through the rings of fire, perform tricks and pull the carousel. With a stab of sadness, he suddenly remembered the last circus. The moving carousel was forty feet off the ground, too high to be safe and made the horses very nervous. Although he knew lowering it was probably the right thing to do, he did not lower it to the ground. The kids and their families all cheered as the carousel kept spinning faster and faster and the horses grew more and more excited. Suddenly, one horse became terrified and jumped. He just lay there with his eyes closed, not moving. The music stopped and the carousel lowered. Everyone ran to the horse's side but came away assuming that there was no hope. A vet was quickly summoned and the horse was taken away on a gurney made just for horses.

Although he was alive, he was badly injured and had to have constant care. His human family gave him warm baths, read to him everyday and fed him his favorite things like carrots, apples and oats with honey. He is happy now that he is well and has love but is grateful that he will never again have to ride the carousel.

By Saturday evening, the farmer was very worried. He had searched high and low and could not find the horses. The circus had packed up and left the village but the horses were taking no chances... they remained hidden. Ben had been standing guard at the mouth of the crater and could hear the farmer calling to them but he pretended not to notice. He had told the others that they would return to the barn on Sunday because by that time, they would need more food and water; for now, they knew the farmer would pace and worry and worry and worry.

OH WOH IS HE...

There once lived a man named Woh...Woh's name was Daniel Wohlers but no one seemed to remember anything other than Woh. Woh had an insatiable thirst for all things miserable. Woh wanted to be smart; in fact, he wanted to be a scientist but Woh could not stop worrying about the high cost of school or travel or weather or dry cleaning or UFOs or pigeon droppings or anything else that Woh thought he should worry about.

Woh lived under a very dark cloud...he could not see the sunshine because each time the sun would peek out from underneath the clouds, Woh would re-position himself so that the ray of light would miss him. His blanket of woes was so heavy that many times he would give up before the thought ever occurred to him to try. Woh was a very troubled man.

One night, Woh had a dream. He dreamed that he was inside of a tent and all four sides had collapsed. The top of the tent was also beginning to fall. When Woh woke up, he could not remember why he was in the tent in the first place. Woh thought it was

In the Garden of Moonlight

because he'd had a bit of libation before going to sleep, to help him forget what a miserable day he'd had. He finally decided that in his alcohol-induced dementia, someone must have demolished his tent while he slept, if it had been a tent at all...last he remembered, he had been asleep in his own bed.

Woh was simply delirious with worry so his mind conjured up all manner of wrong things that were happening to him, when in fact, Woh was so worried that there would be nothing for him to worry about that he simply lost his will to live a normal life. So Woh wandered the streets, pondering the enormity of his burden. He walked until he came to a small dirt road which looked forlorn but slightly interesting so he followed it. Woh didn't notice that the sunlight and the sidewalks had ended and there was nothing but dirt underfoot and trees towering overhead. Woh had walked into the forest. Still he continued walking until he could go no farther...his walk ended at a river. High above him, he heard the musical singing of birds which seemed to match the rhythm of his pounding heart.

The ground here was damp and a bit spongy. Woh stared into the water and worried if the damp ground would ruin his shoes. The currents were swift and there was a lot of driftwood floating by. Woh wanted to grab a piece as it floated by but worried what would happen if he actually caught it...what would happen if he rode it to the end of the line or where the river meets the? Woh could not decide where the river would end so he worried that he would be too long in the river and would not know what to do.

While Woh pondered his fate, it grew late and soon it was too dark to find his way out of the forest. There was a moon but it was mostly hidden by the trees so there was very little light. Woh was not afraid of the dark but he worried that he should be because all manner of scary things wander the forest at night and Woh had no weapon. So now Woh just stood and stared into the river, with the driftwood passing by and the moon slowly rising and the wind singing in the trees and the frogs and crickets beginning their nightly serenade and could not decide what to do. Woh was so weighed down with worry that he completely lost tract of time.

When I woke up, I knew right away that things had changed in my life. The first thing I noticed was that I was in the water, clinging to a piece of driftwood as clouds scudded across the moon. I don't remember getting into this river, or whatever body of water this might be, and I can think of no reason why a sane person would be here in the first place. So maybe I am not sane. Am I dead and is this the hereafter? Far in the distance, I heard the bells of a church clanging. Then I heard the hooting of an owl not too far away.

The second thing that grabbed my attention was that I'm soaking wet and my head hurts something awful. It has this incessant thumping like a bass drum and the thumping was getting louder and much more intense as the angry water swirled around me. My mouth tastes like the inside of a carburetor and I feel as dizzy as a tumbleweed. Panic was beginning to creep into my brain. If this is the hereafter, I would like to skip it altogether and get back to the routine stuff of regular mundane living...at the moment, I cannot recall what that was like.

I suppose the first order of business is to get off this piece of wood and get out of the water. It's cold and my pippies are freezing. The trees are rushing past faster and faster as the current picks up speed. I can see the bank but got no clue how to get there from here. I will surely drown if I leave this precarious perch on my piece of driftwood.

I started to pray but suddenly thought

that after all of these years, do I really know how? Will there still be someone listening to me? While I pondered this deep and disturbing dilemma, I was suddenly slammed into a boulder the size of Aruba. I was deposited not so gently on this rock and knocked unconscious or perhaps I only imagined that I was unconscious. While I was having this out-of-body experience, I was also having a conversation with a very large creature from the depths of the river or the dark depths of my water-logged imagination. He had golden eyes, a long snout, several sets of very sharp teeth and a tongue that must have been two feet long. It flicked over very large, sharp, brown-tinted teeth and he was asking if I was enjoying the view. I had no ready response, just stared in amazement. He was saying to me that the river is usually wild this time of the year and no place for a novice. He was telling me that the time had come to get on with the business of living instead of worrying about everything that hardly requires thought, let alone worry. He was explaining to me that I was going to be given a choice…to get on his back and that he would take me safely to the bank of the river or that he would gladly crush me like a pineapple, swallow me whole and I would have no more reason to worry ever again.

I was cold, wet, hungry, sleep-deprived and surely delirious. I was out in the middle of a raging river having a conversation with a river creature, and he was giving me life advice. At that moment, either I woke up and reality was too much for me to process or I simply made the decision to take the chance to get on his back and get out of this freezing water. I gave no thought to there being a third option but I could almost hear the beads of sweat as they lined up and gave chase down my cold wet spine.

I must have made an attempt to crawl onto the creature's back because suddenly there was an awful splashing as I held on for dear life. I was sailing across the water in the direction of the trees. When we reached the bank, I was unceremoniously dumped on the ground. Strange and otherworldly shadows seemed to slither across me as I lay on the ground. Minutes which felt like days seemed to pass as I attempted *to climb to my feet. The river creature gave me a wicked smile and told me to follow the trail and that it would take me toward the highway and from there, someone would help me find my way back home. He then bid me adieu and told me he would not like to see me again, but if I found my way back to the river, we would surely do lunch, not much to my enjoyment, only his. I gave him a limp soggy wave and began my stumbling shivering way through the trees.*

Woh is now safely back with the family he had forgotten that he had, even a son whom he had named Dan Wohlers Jr. but decided to change his name to Wynne, a much better name for a boy who will have a happy and successful life free of worry.

When your woes are dark and heavy and your troubles are more than few...have a chat with Dr. Gator...he will straighten things out for you...

The Wilted Wisdom of Cee McAdams

TRACK OF THE KOOKABURRA

It was a cold December day, dark ominous clouds, hanging low...a day full of the promise of bad news and a lurking disaster. I checked my bedside clock and it told me it was nearly 9 A.M....I've got to do something about this lying clock...I only just got to sleep about an hour ago. I dragged myself out from underneath my blanket, went into the bathroom to splash some cold water on my face, just to get the blood flowing so I could get my eyes open all the way. You're probably guessing that I am not much of a morning person...you would be correct. Considering what's in store for me today, I may prove to be not   much of an afternoon person either.

I was on the case of an incoming shipment, a real work of art. I had been notified that it was on its way but not yet at its destination so I waited by the phone with baited breath for further developments. And then I waited some more. I finally had to make a move. I called the first person on the list who had knowledge of my shipment but he knew nothing...he put me on hold while he checked his paperwork. Then I heard his voice telling me that it was in route and had been in route days before that. I inquired as to it origin, the north pole? Otherwise, how could it take this long to get here!

I waited several more minutes while there was more paper-shuffling and then a new voice was in my ear. At the end of that exchange, I felt as if I was in a burlesque show with some old 1930's comedians performing the comedy routine 'who's on first...' no one knew 'who' and I very much doubt they knew 'why' and 'how' had left the game... the ambiguity was indeed comical... Kookaburra thought so and began to laugh.

I had been given several names and numbers to call , hoping to find someone with knowledge of what had happened to my shipment. So far, I had been told it was here...it was in-transit...it was misplaced...it had been stored in a new place...the person in charge had to find the right size truck on which to load it...it had been loaded on a truck... the truck had been hijacked by Elves ...the truck has now been found and returned but was on a flat...my shipment was where it always was and had not been moved for several days. Confusion was running rampant! I hardly knew what to believe! I wanted to crawl back underneath my blanket and wait for another day but unfortunately, that was not a good option. I had to get to the bottom of this comedy of errors, hopefully today but it was already late...the evening sun was sinking so I knew there would be no more deliveries today. The clock was ticking and my patience was plummeting.

Troubled and anxiety-ridden, I lay across the bed and starred at the ceiling, hoping that inspiration would assert itself. I actually fell asleep, probably from a severe case of dry eye. When I awoke, it was already the next day and my frustration was boiling at a new high. If only I had a better friendship with Jim Beam, I could have skipped all of this and in a matter of minutes, my troubles would have melted away or poured themselves down the drain, but I never developed a love affair with Jim or Jack or any of the other men of hard liquor fame, so after much pondering and no light bulbs lit up, I got out of bed and called the shipper one last time. This time I spoke with a completely different person who insisted on begging my pardon because she had only just entered the fray and was trying to play catchup. She then went into her spiel about someone dropping the ball and that I should have been notified so that an appointment could have been set... since that was not done, the shipment could not be loaded and a driver dispatched. In addition to that, someone had called and requested a change of delivery address but their go-between had not provided that address and they were still awaiting that paperwork. OH MY GREAT JOY!

By now, I'm all but shouting into the phone, accusing her and all of her colleagues of gross incompetence. I could tell that she was exerting great effort, trying not to use a few really colorful words ...instead, she transferred me to her manager. I continued screaming into the phone....Kookaburra unabashedly was laughing his head off.

After an eternity of waiting, the manager, using calm that I very much doubt he was feeling, assured me that my shipment would reach me today...just please give him a little time to round up a bobtail. I hung up the phone, swore at Kookaburra, but he only laughed.

About an hour later, someone called to ask me if I could avail myself for a delivery, to the original destination...of course I could and off I went. I arrived just in time to see the truck turn the corner. The driver, nervous but friendly, was a slightly larger version of the Grinch who stole Christmas but without the green aura. He issued forth more apologies but soon, we were opening doors and cranking levers and at last my shipment was delivered into my custody. I thanked him for all of his hard work in getting it loaded and with a wave and a smile, he bid me a safe holiday and I returned the good wishes.

I drove across town on a cloud and with a smile on my face, anxious to see this work of art that had caused me so much stress. I parked in my driveway and opened it with a flourish and was rewarded with a feeling of OH WOW! It was magnificent! Even Kookaburra was impressed and has at last stopped laughing hysterically.

IN THE SHADOW OF EVIL

Introduction

My name is Russha Fethersteen. I wish I could tell you that I always had a wonderfully easy and happy life. I wish I could tell that I always knew or felt, that something was not quite right in the heart and mind of one of my children and that I knew that one day I would die of a broken heart. But I cannot or will not tell you any of this. I suppose I should have known and tried to circumvent this tragedy, but I didn't see it or acknowledge it in time to save myself. I had plenty of previews but I suppose one could say I was in a kind of 'passive denial.'

My husband of 50 plus years kept me insulated from most of the wrongs surrounding our daily lives and so I was not inclined to even suspect that this person had been plotting and scheming... always had a devious plan imprinted on his warped and diseased brain, to get rid of his parents [and siblings] so that he could get control of a parcel

In the Garden of Moonlight

of land that he called his, so that he would have a place to lie down and a roof over his head, none of it did he have to work or pay for, but eventually he would claim unlawful ownership.

By the time you finish reading this account, based on actual events, you will believe that this individual walked out of or was shoved out of hell...it is the story of pure evil and how the intertwined characteristics of both animal and human personalities manifested themselves, especially in this one pseudo human being.

In the Shadow of Evil

It was a cold December day. Just how cold I had no way to tell for sure. The thermostat inside was not a good indication of how cold it was outside but my old bones had a way of announcing weather changes especially if it meant cold or damp weather was on the way. The morning was not too bad but I knew that night was going to be even colder. Winter had roared in with bluster and a bad attitude. He had flexed his muscles and puffed out his cheeks and the temperature had started dropping. By late afternoon, the sky was completely devoid of the sun and the few clouds still hanging around looked dreary and crestfallen.

I had long since left the confines and comfort of my rustic home and was by now living with one my children. Contrary to popular belief, living with one of my children was not the ideal situation that I had imagined it would be. I was alone more often than not and spent a lot of my days just puttering around the house, trying to find something to occupy my time and my mind, but every now and then, reality would set in and I would find myself on the verge of panic.

In the Garden of Moonlight

My friends, the few that were left, were not in the city so I felt somewhat disconnected here. There was not much for me to do on my own and depended on one of the children to take me grocery shopping or to church or to whatever events that he or she thought I might enjoy. Other times, I was alone, more often than not. At night was probably the worse. I would hear all manner of strange sounds, not like those I was used to hearing around my former home. I knew that those sounds were made by the two-legged creatures who were most likely up to no good, as far as I was concerned, very unlike the furry creatures who had no harmful intent; still I tried to settle in and not worry too much...I knew someone would be coming back sooner or later.

When I was first invited to come and live with this child, I was so elated that it made me slightly dizzy... it took a fair amount of willpower not to jump up and down...I had never lived alone before and just the thought of it was a bit disorienting. I thought I was going to be as happy as a clam but as the days and nights crept by and I was alone so much of the time, those euphoric moments evaporated like a small puddle on a hot day. I spent too much time remembering my late husband...those feelings and thoughts reverberated in my head, and some days, I would almost hear his voice but could not quite make out the words. Sometimes that rolling undulation of memory felt blissful but at other times, sadness would consume me and I would dissolve in tears. Having no one around to talk to most of the time, the loneliness would simply overwhelm me. I would watch TV for entertainment and there was always plenty of food for me to eat but somehow, I had the notion that being here would be very different... little did I know that my world was about to take a drastically wrong turn.

On this particular morning, I was sitting at the kitchen table trying to decide if I wanted to make breakfast for myself or just have a cup of coffee, finally deciding that a steaming bowl of oatmeal would do the trick. I was feeling a bit chilled and wanted to dial up the heat but realized that I had no knowledge of such thinks as furnaces and fancy thermostats...I was going to have to call someone for help so I dialed a number, grabbed a heavier robe and settled down to wait. Looking back, I realize now that that call was the beginning of the end.

When he finally decided that he could not find the furnace or turn the heat up or know how do anything that would make me more comfortable, he offered to take me to his house. I was cold and had not a clue that I was the lamb, voluntarily going to the slaughter. He is what you would get if you could cross a venomous snake with a vulture. He is a creature who hates to work, who

In the Garden of Moonlight

profits from the suffering of others, who is greedy, crafty and devious...he avoids volatile situations because he is mostly a spineless coward...he is opportunistic and therefore he relishes preying on the weak, the dead or the dying...he is a being who is not threatened by criticism...he is usually confident, enigmatic, shrewd, insidious, parasitic, ruthless and cold-bloodied. He is mostly simple but can make complex decisions when it comes to his own survival. He is callous, and unwilling to accept blame. So why would I have gone along with this creature? I should have stopped long enough to think this through but I was ignorant, totally unaware and cold, so I packed a small overnight bag and went along. I really wanted to be warm again.

It would be several days before I would learn that some monsters don't crawl out of the swamp or hide underneath the bed. I know that some monsters come out of the fantasies of parents who want to scare their children so they will go to sleep on demand, but some monsters are of such rare breed and cunning that you have no reason to suspect that they are ready and willing to slice open your throat and leave you to die a slow but horrific death. This particular breed of monster was the disciplined kind that would rather watch you die in small increments and show no remorse because even if he was not a supremely gifted sociopath, he was at the very least a ruthless one when it came to getting what he wanted. Much to my horror, I learned that he had no more feelings for me as his mother than he would have had for a painted rock or a pine tree. I learned the hard and painful truth but much too late to save myself an enormous amount of disappointment, heartache and financial ruin.

My husband [of more than 50 years] came home one day after being out in the pasture looking after the livestock. His face was scratched and he look a bit disheveled. I asked what had happened and he told me that he had fallen...just tipped right over, no rhyme or reason that he knew about at the time. He said that he felt OK, just a little embarrassed but thankfully no one saw him take a tumble. The episodes of falling continued until one a particular day, a friend was visiting and upon finding him on the ground unable to right himself, helped him up and back to the house... we decided then and there that it was time to get help. I called some of the children and collectively, they wanted to take him to the hospital right away. He strongly objected on the grounds that, in his mind, doctors wanted to rush old people away before it was their time...this was his way of stating that he had a fear of doctors, real or imagined.

Long hours later, the children insisted so off he went to the hospital and we soon learned that he had one those neuro-muscular diseases for which there was no cure. The doctors basically had no recommendations for us, no medication that would help, only that the long-term outlook was not a positive one, so they dismissed him and

In the Garden of Moonlight

we just took him home to begin the long regimen of trying to make him as comfortable as possible, at least most of us did. Each of us had a particular chore of bathing, or feeding or shaving or being the companion. One of us should have been the sentry.

One day not too long after my husband came home from the hospital, we found this person with his hand around my husband's throat, slowly squeezing the life out of him. My husband was by now, growing weaker and could not fight him off but thankfully one of the other children walked in just in time. He over-heard some very strange angry words such as 'you're not going to need it where you're going.' He was trying to force my husband to tell him where he had money hidden in the house and where the ownership papers could be found. Mostly he was demanding to have everything signed over to him. Needless to say, this was not accomplished but from that day forward, until the angels came to take my husband away, he was never left alone even for a minute, while this creature was around.

This assault and act of cowardice left us all bewildered...we were constantly picking our chins up from the floor, almost in total disbelief...no one really understood. How could he do such a thing to his father who was by that time, unable to talk or defend himself? A few days later, my husband handed me a piece of paper on which he had written a message...he had figured things out. The note stated that this individual had been sent by 'the devil' and warned me to watch out for him. At that time, I was surrounded by other children and didn't take this as a warning...I have now lived to regret it.

My husband left me with land, enough money to survive and a house already paid off and well furnished. It was not the lap of luxury, not many amenities, but it was home. The problem with this was that I would have had to live alone, far away from anyone that I knew and far from medical care facilities. I never learned to drive and depended on my husband for almost everything including the day to day management of the place and paying of all the bills. We had a simple but comfortable life. I could travel to see my children and other family members whenever I had the hankering and my husband would provide me with funds. Now that he is gone, I am like the proverbial fish out of water and literally drowning in air, trying to learn to deal with this new and strange existence. Of course, I had no plans to lose my husband...I just assumed that he would always be there to take care of things...the angels came and took him away before I was prepared for him to leave. Now I have found myself in the lair of this parasite and I didn't know if it would have done me any good to be afraid...thinking back, it was probably fear that kept me so cold and uncomfortable. Truthfully, I totally lacked the wherewithal to understand that bizarre creature...he was the blood of my blood but I could hardly believe it.

One day, approximately 1 week after I moved in with him, I was lying in bed looking up at the ceiling, and wondered why the paint was cracked and why he had not painted this room...I had noticed that other parts of the house needed painting as well when my wool-gathering was interrupted by a knock on the door. I cleared my throat and said give me a minute, stretched and then headed for the door. He stood there, looking as forlorn as a snail but said nothing at first, as if choosing just the right, or the wrong words to use. Finally, he asked to be included on my checking account so that he could help me manage my finances...he even offered to go and pay the taxes on my home so that I would not have to worry about going back and forth to the tax office or even the post office. Something stirred inside my stomach, not too much of a jangle but a definite mild disturbance. I pushed it aside. At the time, his request didn't seem like such an outrageous one since I knew that the money was available and all that needed to be done was to send a check. Unfortunately for me, what appeared to be a lagniappe was wrapped in slimy loincloth and I was about to be stripped naked. At that moment, I was as naïve as a newborn, having forgotten the previous warning. My lack of education and sophistication was about to cost me everything I had.

In the Garden of Moonlight

But I digress. I couldn't possibly spend the rest of my life trying to remember if there were any indication of this person evolving and becoming the inhuman thing that he was or whether or not my husband had ever seen any obvious signs and simply failed to point them out to me. He had tried at least once but that acorn was not heavy enough to fully get my attention. It certainly should have given me a hint of how to I should have side-stepped a collision with this monster, but I was already his prey and he was about to inflict a debilitating would...but he was going to make me suffer first.

Although it's a little too late, I can clearly remember that he never liked work of any sort and would spend hours hiding out in order to avoid doing even the simplest chores. I recall also that he had a penchant for catching and torturing small animals, especially cats, holding them under water to see how long it would take for them to stop breathing. He tried this form of torture with other small animals like toads but cats seemed to have been his favorite, I think because they made loud noises and fought to stay alive. This must have really fueled his already developing proclivity to inflict misery, maiming and eventually killing to satisfy his thirst for maximum destruction.

I can't imagine how I missed it or did I simply choose to ignore the horrifying picture that was developing right before my eyes? I definitely remember seeing the body of a small white kitten floating on the surface of the stock pond and hearing him say that 'that one didn't take long enough.' It gave me a chill like ice water running down my spine even then. His earlier exploits seemed to have prepared him for this new and malicious mission...he has now morphed into this perfectly soulless, fang-bearing monster.

I had been in his lair for about 5 months. The weather was warmer and the breezes were cooler by then and I was no longer cold from the low temperatures, but I was uncomfortable all the time from the environment in his house...his treatment of me left me feeling cold, empty and feeling useless. He seemed carved from stone as he showed me no sign of familiarity, let alone affection. I didn't get as much consideration as a dirty dinner plate.

I inquired almost daily about the taxes and how much was left in my account, but he continued to tell me that the money was gone and that the government had taken it. He failed to explain to me whether or not the taxes had been paid or why the government would have taken my money. I attempted to ask other people and my other children who told me that the bank would not do such a thing without explanation, but they were otherwise of no help since he had custody of my check book and refused to return it to me.

I was fortunate or unlucky as it were, to be there alone when the mail came one day and I was able to get a look at my account statement. Much to my horror and dismay, I discovered that I had a total $18.00 and change left in an account which

In the Garden of Moonlight

had a previous balance of over $6000 when he has asked to pay my taxes for me. As usual, he was smarter and a more gifted liar than most, more cunningly vicious than anyone else and did not provide me with satisfactory answers. There was no one I could go to for help.

I was not the most social person but once in a while, company would have been a good thing. Just to have someone to chat with about church matters, since he would not allow me to attend services, would have been welcomed relief from the solitude, but he did not allow others to come to visit me at his lair. I was cut off from everyone, totally at his mercy of which there was none.

One day he informed me that we would have to leave because the house was being foreclosed. This was a new word and a new concept for me so of course I had no clue what he meant. He then told me that he was several months behind on his payments and that there was no more money for electric, water and other bills and that we would have to get out. He then casually announced that he would be moving into my house but there would be no need for me to go.

Something very cold, like a large sliver of ice, began running around inside my chest and my heart constricted. I felt as if I had been kicked in the belly by a really ticked-off Missouri mule. I had no money, very little food, and no place to go. I felt sick. He had obviously stolen all of my money, used it for his own needs including preparing my own house for his convenience and was throwing me out on the street with nothing but the few clothes I had brought with me to his lair. I couldn't call a taxi or anyone else because the phone was off and besides that, I could not pay the taxi driver anyway. I was alone, helpless, humiliated and destitute. I was in the grips of a screaming depression with my insides rolling and twisting around on itself. I didn't know what else to do so in the depths of my despair, I sat down and cried; for what seemed like hours, huge throbbing sobs escaped without my ability to control them.

I was hungry. I couldn't remember when I had eaten last but I knew there wasn't much food left in the house. My eyes were puffy and my face felt mis-shapened. I knew I had to find someplace to go...I could not stay here and didn't want to be here one minute longer. I certainly could not be out on the street, not in this city where unimaginable things could happen to me. I knew very few people and no one but him knew where I was. Finally, I decided to walk across the street and ask the lady I had seen earlier if she could call someone for me or possibly take me to the house of one of my other children. At first, she only

In the Garden of Moonlight

stared at me as if I were a bright blue alien, then she smiled at me and nodded. I nearly fainted with relief when she agreed to drive me across town. I didn't know the address where I wanted to go but thankfully, I knew how to get there.

I was back at the home of a child whom honestly, I never felt much affection for...it should have been a horrible way for a mother to think about one of her children but frankly, this child never had much affection for me either. She was a difficult child who always lived on the brink of being defiant. If one could cross an elephant with an owl, you would get this child. She was always wise beyond her years...she was independent and loyal to those she felt deserving of her loyalty, mostly her Dad. She was also perceptive, tuned in to things beyond the eyes and ears of the rest of us. She always insisted on solving her own problems and was what I would call 'always in her own head.' She was a solitary child and I thought this to be a bit disconcerting. As a grownup, she gave me both raised eyebrows and elevated blood pressure, plus fits of confusion and a few sleepless nights. This was her house and the same house I had left only months before. I realized what a horrible mistake I had made by leaving because upon my return, I discovered that she had other family members living with her and there was no longer any room for me. There was no place for me to sleep for even one night, so I had to gather the rest of my belongings and go and find another place to stay.

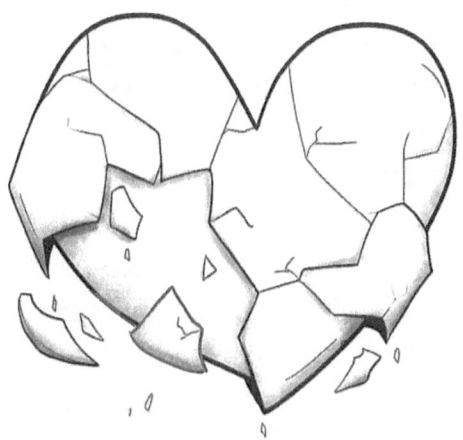

I arrived at the abode, the dwelling, of another son...I hesitate to describe it as a house. This was hardly where I had intended to end up but I was left with no other available options...it was either here or sleep in the street...I didn't even own a car. I suppose there was the possibility of a shelter but I knew nothing about shelters and would not have had the wherewithal to even inquire about them. So, I moved in with this son who had given up his home a few months earlier just so that he could be away from me. I was in fear that he would not accept me but he was kind and showed me in. Over the next several days, he tried his best to make me feel welcomed and to make me as comfortable as possible...this was so much more than I had expected or deserved.

The first two or three days of being there, I had nothing but headaches, bellyaches and bad dreams. I was homeless and as poor as a church mouse. Just the thought of it gave me heart palpitations. My heart would race as if it was trying to get away from me. I would take aspirin to try to ease the throbbing headaches but that fixed nothing. It was such a small place that I couldn't even pace more than a few feet before I would bump into a wall or a piece of furniture. I wanted to talk about what had happened but I was too ashamed; besides, who would I tell and would anyone even begin to believe the rantings of an old woman...the whole business was draining and exhausting. It was hard to keep from crying...that would only have upset everyone else. I would lay on the bed and close my eyes. My mind would drift one way and then another and somehow it drifted to the memory of my older son.

I remembered that the older son, who reminded me of an otter, always preening, had to fix that one stubborn curl that was out of place. He was quite narcissistic and would tend to be controlling. When that didn't work for him, he could become verbally abusive...he had no use for logic. Despite all of that, he was mine, the love of my life and he had been taken away too soon, leaving a crater in my heart. He had also been a victim of this soulless creature. He had been sick for a long while and near the end, had become too weak to do much for himself. He had either appointed or simply asked this person to be his representative or just be kind enough to look after things for him should his health deteriorate to the point that he could not take care of things himself. I later learned that he had stolen all of the money in my son's account and had pilfered almost everything that was worth selling from his house. Inquiries were made as to what had happened to one item or another, that gun or that suit and he would always deny having any knowledge of anything. Of course, no one saw him take anything...he hardly wanted a captive audience while he was helping himself to things that did not belong to him, so he made his 'visits' in the early morning hours when there were no witnesses to point fingers at him.

Just remembering all of this made me woozy and I would be assaulted by stronger and more intense headaches. As soon as they would ease a bit, I would again be overwhelmed with the hopelessness that had become my life. I would close my eyes and my world would slide into this incomprehensible nightmare of being thrown into a ditch.

I am not far from the highway or some type of major thoroughfare. I can hear cars and trucks going by at a high rate of speed...I can even smell the exhaust fumes, but apparently, I'm in a ditch too deep or too far away for anyone to see me. I'm not sure why but I have the feeling that it is someplace out in a rural area. I can hear animal sounds like horses whinnying and cows mooing. I will sometimes get the comfortable sensation of being on the back of a hay wagon being pulled by a tractor like in the days of my youth. I am never here long enough for the sun to rise or for night to fall...I am always in a nether world that is neither day or night.

I sometimes feel cold and then feel things climbing over me, sometimes very slowly, sometimes squirming and other times things will scuttle as if in a great hurry to get wherever they are going. I look around but I can never see anything; there is always shadow but I cannot see the sun. I feel as if I'm drifting in and out of consciousness but it's hard to tell...in this nether world, time seems to stand still.

Just to amuse myself, I sometimes have conversations with whatever happens to be passing by, usually a tarantula, but he complains that he has things to do and places to go and has no time for idle chatter or he will miss out on the wonderful meal that just wabbled by...perhaps he will have time to chat on his way back.

I must have gotten distracted by my deep and tantalizing conversation with the spider because suddenly I hear

In the Garden of Moonlight

a car coming... it must be just beneath the hill. I can feel the ground vibrating beneath me and know that it's close. Then there are lights in my face and hands lifting me up. I open my eyes and find that I am back at the house of my son. It seems that I was always in the ditch 3 days or perhaps three days and nights each time, the best I can calculate, then someone finds me and return me to this house.

This son is what one would think of if you could cross a doctor with a sloth. He is slow of movement, slow to anger, slow to act...he is kind, patient, gentle and not known for his sharp sense of anything...he tends to see things in black and white and takes life one moment at a time...he is not very good at planning ahead...he tends to veer off the beaten path usually to the detriment of himself...he is usually [a good friend to have] but always a good son.

From my bedroom, I could look out of the window and see nothing but raggedy weeds, dying grass, the rear of a few houses and the remnants of what used to be a farm. The place is rundown, poorly ventilated and in very poor condition. The floor is unlevel but my son has put carpet on the floor in the room where I was sleeping. The room that used to be the living room had become his tack room, full of old leather parts, bits and pieces of bridles, broken tools, several sizes of nails and screws, old buckets and mostly rotten rope, torn and tattered beyond use. There was even a wood stove, long since broken and beyond use. At one place near the rear of the house, you could see right through the walls into the backyard. The fence was mostly falling down and the roof long since needed replacing. Home sweet home! I was going to have to get used to the idea, and soon.

The truth is, this place was dilapidated and should have been demolished several years before, but I was thankful that I had a son with enough human kindness to offer me a bed to sleep in and a roof over my head, so I tried to settle in but spent most of my days just sitting, staring out of the window, twittling my thumbs and feeling sorry for myself. Some days, I wanted to cook for him but his kitchen left much to be desired, no cooktop or even useful cooking utensils...I didn't trust what he had for an oven but I learned to 'make do' and tried not to complain. Thankfully he had a lady friend with a car and would drive to the store or restaurant for most of what we ate without having to do much cooking. I discovered pizza, fish sandwiches and fried chicken that came in a box! I even learned that the chicken was better than I could make myself.

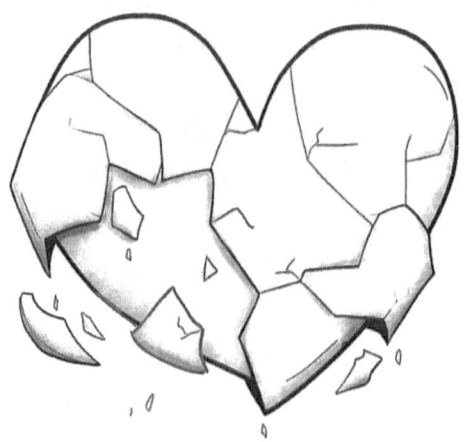

When my husband and I first started out, we had nothing but two pair of hands and two young strong bodies...not a dollar between us. We lived in a place with four corners...if one had a lot of imagination, you could have called it a house with four rooms, or space for four small rooms. We had curtains made from flour sacks and linoleum on the floor, but it was cracked in more places than not. We lived in fear that things that squirmed or slithered would pay us a visit while we slept, things that would crawl in from underneath. I would awake every morning and check each possible hiding place for unwanted visitors. Other than a bug or a millipede, I never got any nasty surprises.

I suppose you could say that we lived close to the soil, but we also lived close to the sun for very long hours and was up close and personal with hunger a lot. We cleared bushes and pulled up stumps to make room for planting. We got to know several mosquitos by their first names and knew some of them by the songs they played incessantly in our ears. We destroyed mounds, rousted raccoons and scared off snakes. We mostly worked from early just as the sun was making its arrival to late in the evening when the shadows grew long and the last rays of orange sherbet was melting into the horizon. We would stumble into the house, barely alive, and eat whatever was available to us, then fall into bed half dead. We worked long and hard and finally got 20 acres of our own paid for and later we were able to add a few more. We plowed...we sweated...we planted...quitting or giving up were not options available to us.

We grew most of what we ate but it never seemed to be enough. There were always more people to feed than there was food...most of those people didn't belong in our house but who just could not seem to have homes of their own or get jobs or do anything except beg and bum from those of us who worked like trojans. They would show up just when they thought we had picked or pulled or gathered or dressed, depending on what was in season. They knew that they would have a nice free meal without having to work for it.

My husband was a Christian and a charitable man, always trying to help, willing to share what he could with others although we barely had enough for ourselves. I screamed and cussed about it but in the end, I lost the argument more often than not. I only wanted those bums to see the outside of my door, preferably with the help of a large muddy boot.

My husband had a real knack for growing things

but he had an amazing head for business. He would often say that if only he could get his hands on a few head of cattle, he could do some bigger and better things. One day he announced to me that he would speak to a friend of his about advancing him enough money to buy a few head and he would pay him back when he sold the calves in the spring. This sounded like a pipe dream to me but then I knew nothing about business and could do nothing but pray that it worked out.

Many years and seven kids later, we had a better place we called home and even had a little money put aside for emergencies. And I do mean a little. There were always open hands ready and willing to clean us out if we had let it be known that we had even one cent that we didn't have to use for ourselves. Raising seven kids during those times was especially hard but mostly nobody cared about our struggles or what we needed as long as we were willing to pass something over to them. Now all of these years later, after all of the work, sweat and sacrifice to have this home and this land, there is this one last creature (I hesitate to refer to him as a person) who did not feel that it was his duty to do any of the work, actually felt obliged to do anything and everything he could to avoid working, has robbed me blind and taken away what was mine.

When a mother has [seven] children, she tells herself that she knows right away which child will be special, which one will give her the most problems and which ones will give her more proud moments. I had heard from older generations that when there is a family of more than one child, the mother has a favorite and the father may have a favorite of his own. On rare occasions, the parents will have the same favorite, but that was not the case in this family. As each child came along, I tried to figure out which one would do what or be what kind of child but all I was able to figure out was that they were all as different from each other as golden retrievers are from elephants or as different as ants are from otters.

Looking back, I suppose I felt some little twinge, or thought that I knew that one was different from the others and not for any of the usual reasons. He didn't have three heads, or an extra eye or even three sixes tattooed on his body. He didn't do banshee-like keening or bay at the moon, but I suspected that something was not quite right. There were times when I would feel ripples on my skin like miniature tidal waves whenever he would be near me...the hair on the back of my neck would stand on end. I could see nothing strange... he looked totally normal. I had no explanation for why I had to sometimes muffle a scream or wanted to flee from the room to put distance between him and me, even for a moment. Now realization has reared its ugly head...it took Satan a few years but he has finally come to take possession and complete control of his own.

Even when a mother knows something is abnormal, her instincts are to prepare to take on any threat to her or her children; she surely should feel immune to fear when it comes to one of her own children. A mother has this bravado, which is often false but she is reluctant to give those feelings a voice for fear that they may come true...now I realize that I should have spoken out loudly, clearly and often...maybe then we could have considered sending him to Tibet to live with the monks...maybe then we could have saved ourselves and possibly could have given him a chance to be more normal...and just maybe none of this would have happened to me...I could have been spared this unbelievable nightmare.

Even though I say this now, I never really believed that even the monks could have made any real difference in the mind of this child...he was born without a soul. He had no conscience. The monks would have been hard-pressed to know where to begin to help, guide or change him. I shudder to think what would have happened once he arrived in Tibet...I suspect that he would have taken to drowning or suffocating the baby yaks or one of the monks would have been found hanging limp in his own robe.

There were definitely signs that I chose to ignore. Something very dark and evil was taking shape inside of him. For instance, he never liked other kids nor did he like any of the animals on the place. He hated the chickens...he said they looked at him funny. Wild turkeys would wander onto our place and we had a few of our own but they mostly stayed out of his way...because he couldn't catch them, he would just throw rocks at them. He complained that the livestock 'smelled bad' plus they were too large for him to bully and required too much of something known as 'work' just having to drive them toward the corral, but he would throw rocks at the small ones whenever he could get away with it. He would rather kill the dog than feed him, and did once, and buried it in a dry creek bed. We kept wondering why the dog never came back and finally assumed that he had run away chasing a rabbit or some other kind of critter or perhaps took up residence someplace else. Then one day my husband found the shallow grave...it didn't take long to discover what was buried in it. We questioned the boy about it but he denied having seen the dog or having anything to do with a grave. We had no proof...there was

In the Garden of Moonlight

no smoking gun and no blood spilled...just a very dead family dog. No one had seen him do it, but we had very strong suspicions.

My husband never caught him conducting any of his animal experiments or he would probably not have lived to grow into this full-sized monster... my husband would have had him drawn and quartered. I didn't want to see that happen to him... after all, he was my child...but I was ignorant...he was the damned and I was already doomed...I had an inkling but didn't have a clue what it meant. By the time I got a handle on it, it was too late.

My husband was a good man but not a very patient one. He had no tolerance for 'foolishness' and could not abide laziness. He, like me, had not much formal education so we did not understand words like 'sociopath' and monster. Of course, my husband had no fear other than of things associated with divine power such as lightening, so the strangeness of this boy did not worry him much...the laziness drove him to distraction. Every now and then, he would yell at him to try to get him to do some semblance of work, but after a while, he grew weary of that and basically gave up. He would breathe deeply and let the cool and silent wind cool his temper. In hindsight, I should have allowed him to be drawn and quartered... after all of these years, all I really know for sure is that he is a pseudo human, devoid of all real human feelings and emotions, twisted beyond my ability to understand. I wonder what my husband would say, now that the creature has grown into his truly disturbing soulless self.

Sometime during that summer, I decided to travel to visit one of the other children, a daughter. She was the child who reminded me mostly of a parrot. She was pretty, vocal, a fence-sitter, intelligent, liked attention, liked to talk, loved to be pampered and avoided conflict at all costs. However, she could be manipulative and deceitful. She would usually empty my purse upon my arrival but this time, my purse had already been cleaned out along with my account. This time, I had nothing to give her. It was an odd feeling.

I was pretty much on the verge of totally unravelling and was down on my luck by this time so she had to advance me enough money for an airplane ticket while I waited for my money to start again and then accumulate enough to pay her back...I had learned that I needed to close the previous account post haste and I had done just that.

I spent most of my time just sitting around her house, half of it staring at the TV, half of the time staring at nothing, too depressed to be much of a guest. This daughter liked to shop, loved to spend money as if she could mint it herself. She had a way of spending more than she earned and could never seem to hang on to a dollar for very long. She tried to take me shopping but I

In the Garden of Moonlight

could not feel up to it no matter how much she cajoled or performed delicate arm-twisting. She would take me out to eat but food didn't please me either...I had no pressing need to feel human again. She and her family wanted me to talk about my ordeal and hopefully, if I could just get it out of my system, they felt that maybe I could feel better. I tried once but unfortunately, all that did was knock the scab off and the wound would open again and all of that misery, degradation and shame would pour out. Little did I know at the time, that my little fence-sitter knew all about what had happened and had actually aided and abetted the very monster who had caused all of this pain and misery.

I learned about this betrayal way too late and it was of too little comfort to me near the end... actually, no comfort at all. How does a mother deal with betrayal by not just one but two of her children? I waited in the heavy silence but no answers came to me. I tried not to think about it but I could not switch off my mind. I closed my eyes and found only darkness.

I awoke in a strange place, alone, a hospital room. I couldn't remember when I had arrived nor why I was here or who had brought me. I had no clue where it was...I didn't see the name of the hospital written on anything. I looked around for someone or something familiar but found nothing. I looked out of the window at the fat clouds and the gray sky, but neither the clouds or the sky offered any answers. I felt a little light-headed and a little disoriented at first, but I felt no pain or discomfort and I wondered again why I was here in a hospital. Just for an instance, I felt a strange sensation, the faint smell of peppermint and the feeling that I should have been pale pink instead of teal-blue... the aura was a bit off but mildly exciting. After a long moment, I heard the silence, so with a deep breath and a nod, I left it all behind and went to where I hoped would be a kinder and gentler place.

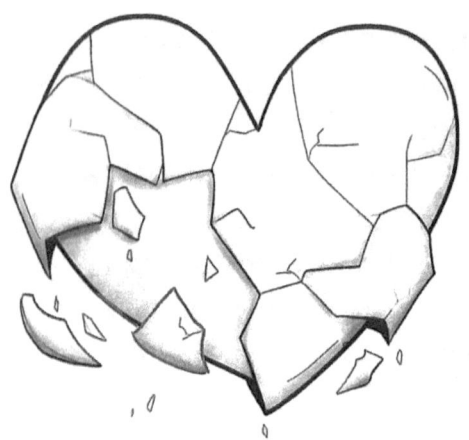

Russha Fethersteen died alone in a hospital far from her home. Neither one of her children was by her bedside. Her death certificate stated 'OF NATURAL CAUSES' ...manner of death: cardiac arrest. It should have stated 'this mother died of a 'desolate spirit and a broken heart.'

When her remains were returned to her home state, she was unloaded from the aircraft and was allowed to sit in a waiting area, in 90 degree plus heat for several hours. The 'thing' who used to be her son just left her there...he had no further use of her.

...and so I write...

Today I sit by my window, watching the shadows from the trees grow longer while reveling in the rhythm of the flute as it reverberates through my soul. It seems that no matter the effort, the day or the time, my mind clings to the image of you standing there in the isle...I get no respite, day or night. I see you everywhere I go so the 'entity' in my mind keeps trying to formulate the most appropriate scenario for actually meeting you, everything from a simple ' hello' to a seductive embrace. All I really wanted so much to do at that moment was run to you and melt in your pocket, but I feared a rebuff. My days are consumed with thoughts of you and my nights are filled with dreams of how much you enhance my life. As long as you insisted on being on my mind, I needed to transfer some of those thoughts and emotions to paper. Sometimes I can easily segue from reality to my fictional world but once ensconced in my world of make-believe, the reverse sometimes requires great effort and concentration and is sometimes unsuccessful...and so I write.

In the Garden of Moonlight

Recently I read a story about a young man who was smitten by a young lady but was too intimidated by your beauty to approach her, so rather than risk allowing her to get away, he summoned his courage and wrote a whimsical poem for her, then read it to her at a time when he felt that she would be his captive audience. After that moment, they became inseparable. Such is my desire, to totally capture your imagination...and so I write...

The day I saw you, I did not have a poem prepared – sadly I don't do poetry - and you were able to escape before I made a fool of myself...but I cannot escape the world built only of my imagination... and so I must write.

Hesitation is truly a cousin of fear but my fear has manifested itself in the form of sweet and sometimes erotic dreams that have no chance of coming true. I can do nothing to quell this fear that I will never see you again and my heart breaks a little. I write about you or rather about what I see in my mind's eye. If I could, I would probably send you roses with syrupy messages but then you would think I'm a stalker and a bit unhinged. I cannot send flowers...and so I write.

It is my fervent hope along with a small prayer, that I will see you again, but if it never happens, I know that we will continue to have this awesome love affair, seething with passion, but only as it exists in the vibrant world of my imagination. I know I must continue to believe or it will leave a bruise on my soul...and so I write.

Not so long ago, I read a fortune cookie insert which said: 'DON'T GIVE UP...THE BEGINNING IS ALWAYS THE HARDEST.' Food for thought indeed...my heart is already doing backward flips at the very thought of at last, the beginning! I will then be able to abruptly transition from the melancholy, throw away those pensive reflections, cast away that crate of tissue that I have stashed beside my bed...I will no longer need to wipe away tears before they can escape down my cheeks. My fractured heart will mend...the longing in my heart, the ache in my soul can then morph into smiles, an outbreak of great joy and I will be able to blossom like a morning glory when it sees the sunrise.

I know I must write but the feel of your hand in mine or the delicious aura of the first embrace or the taste of that first kiss will linger and will surely pause this run-away-train that is this story, our story...but soon I must write again.

Cee McAdams

www.ingramcontent.com/pod-product-compliance
Lightning Source LLC
Chambersburg PA
CBHW030147200626
46812CB00015B/1736